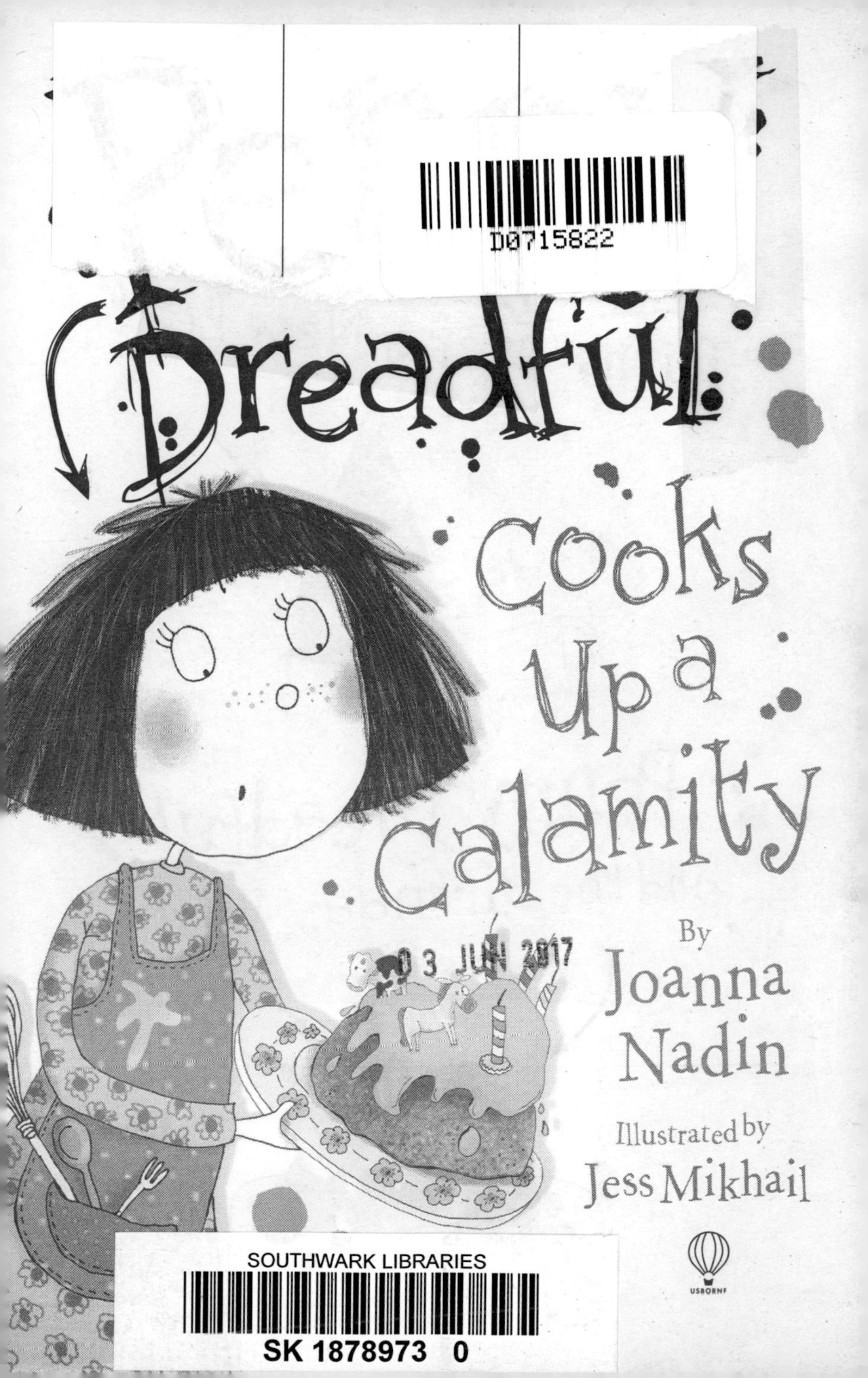

D0715822
03 JUN 2017
SOUTHWARK LIBRARIES
SK 1878973 0

Contents

London Borough of Southwark	
SK 1878973 0	
ASKEWS & HOLT	06-Jul-2012
JF	£4.99

Penny Dreadful Turns Over a New Leaf

My name is not actually Penny Dreadful. It is Penelope Jones.

The "Dreadful" bit is my dad's **JOKE**. I know it is a joke because every time he says it he laughs like a honking goose. But I do not see the funny side. Plus it is not even true that I am dreadful. It is like Gran says, i.e. that I am a **MAGNET FOR DISASTER**.

Mum says if Gran kept a better eye on me in the first place instead of on *Oven Gloves* in the two o'clock at Haydock then I might not be quite so magnetic. But Gran says if Mum wasn't so busy answering phones for Dr. Cement, who is her boss and who has bulgy eyes like hard-boiled eggs (which is why everyone calls him Dr. Bugeye), and Dad wasn't so busy solving crises at the council, then they would be able to solve some crises at 73 Rollins Road, i.e. our house. So you see it is completely not my fault.

But the magnetism is extra-especially annoying when you are trying to **TURN OVER A NEW LEAF**, i.e. not be dreadful **AT ALL**, because it makes it very impossible indeed.

What happens is that me and Gran, and Gran's cat Barry, and my big sister Daisy (who is very irritating), are watching *Animal SOS*, which is a TV series where animals are always nearly dying but then they don't and it is **MIRACULOUS**.

And this week it is all about a dog called Colin who is an **UTTER MENACE** because he is mostly digging holes and burying things in them, e.g.:

1. A pair of red pants

2. A model of Optimus Prime, leader of the Autobots

C. An egg whisk

Only this time he has gone a **STEP TOO FAR** and has tried to bury a toaster under some pansies, only the toaster is still plugged in and he gets an electric shock which makes his hair stand on end like Hugo Brush's, who is in Year Six and who is called "Toilet Brush" (only Mr. Schumann, who is our headmaster, says it is not very **TOLERANT** to call people names, but it was Hugo who started it so that is a complete **CONUNDRUM**).

Anyway, Colin is almost nearly dead and his owner Mrs. McDoon is doing weeping in a red coat, and we are all on the **EDGE OF OUR SEATS** (except Barry who is eating a digestive, even though Mum has told Gran it is **CAT BISCUITS AND CAT BISCUITS ONLY**), when the vet gives Colin a special injection and he **MIRACULOUSLY** doesn't die but sits up and licks a computer. And Griff Hunt, who is the presenter, says he hopes

Colin has learned his lesson, and Mrs. McDoon says he has and he will definitely **TURN OVER A NEW LEAF**. Although this is possibly not true because Colin is looking very much like he wants to bury the computer under the floor. But Griff Hunt ignores this and says Colin is **INSPIRING**, which **IS** true because then we are all very **INSPIRED**, i.e. Gran says she is **TURNING OVER A NEW LEAF** and is not going to let Barry eat digestives any more,

and Daisy says **SHE** is **TURNING OVER A NEW LEAF** and is going to say only Nice Things to people from now on, even to Lucy B. Finnegan, who is normally her best friend (only this week Lucy is best friends with Philippa Rigby-Homerton who has a TV in her bedroom and Mum says no, Daisy cannot have one, not **EVEN** over her dead body).

And I think I would also like to **TURN OVER A NEW LEAF** and it would be quite good not to be shouted at, so I say I am absolutely **NOT** going to be **DREADFUL** any more.

Only Daisy says,

You are an **UTTER MORON** if you think that is going to happen. Pigs are more likely to fly.

But Gran says Daisy's leaf has turned back over already because that was not a Nice Thing, so it is one point to me.

☆ ☆ ☆ ☆

And on Friday it is clear Mr. Schumann has also watched *Animal SOS* because usually he is **SICK AND TIRED** of a lot of things, especially me, e.g.,

Because me and Cosmo Moon Webster, who is my best friend (even though he is a week older than me and a boy), are quite keen on burning things with a magnifying glass, e.g.:

a) An old log
b) A dead ant
3. Bridget Grimes, who is top of the class and Mr. Schumann's favourite

Only today in assembly Mr. Schumann is surprisingly not being **SICK AND TIRED** of me showing Cosmo a gold pirate coin I found outside the post office (only Cosmo says it is not a pirate coin, it is a chocolate sovereign), he is smiling and saying that on Monday in assembly we will be having a special **TALENT SHOW** and anyone can enter, even me.

Which is good because normally I am not allowed onstage because of the time I was Little Lord Jesus in our nativity and did realistic crying, only Bridget Grimes did not think my crying was realistic, she thought it was annoying because no one could hear her sing "Away in a Manger" and so **SHE** started crying, which Mr. Schumann **DID** think was realistic, and also annoying, and also **MY FAULT**.

Anyway, it is completely clear that Mr. Schumann has **TURNED OVER A NEW LEAF**. And I am very **INSPIRED** by this and so is everyone in our class, because when we get back from assembly everyone is shouting like **MAD** about what talents they are going to do in the show, e.g.:

a) Luke Bruce is going to make a poodle out of balloons.

b) Alexander Pringle, who is mostly eating jam sandwiches when he should **NOT** be eating jam sandwiches, is going to show everyone the mole on his leg, which is in the shape of a gnu.

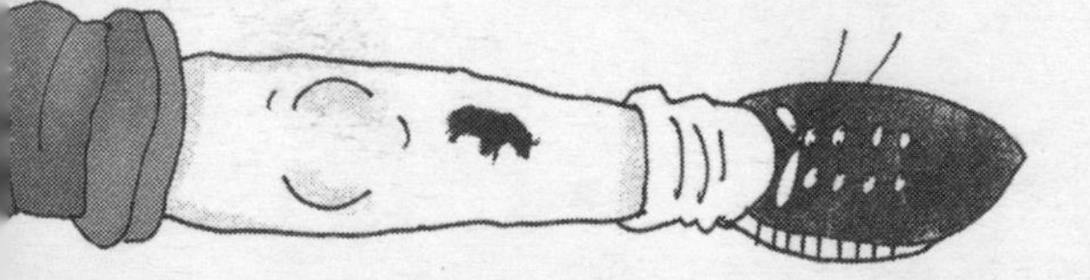

3) Bridget Grimes

is going to play "If I Had A Hammer" on her recorder, and she has not **ONCE** got a note wrong.

d. Cosmo Moon Webster

is going to do a sun dance, because his mum Sunflower (whose real name is Barbara) is not very keen on talent shows because they are **COMMERCIAL** and **COMPETITIVE**, but she **IS** very keen on sun dances.

v) Henry Potts, who is Cosmo's mortal enemy, says he is going to do a rain dance which will **OBLITERATE** Cosmo's sun dance.

6) Cosmo says he is going to do a lightning dance, which will **OBLITERATE** Henry's rain dance.

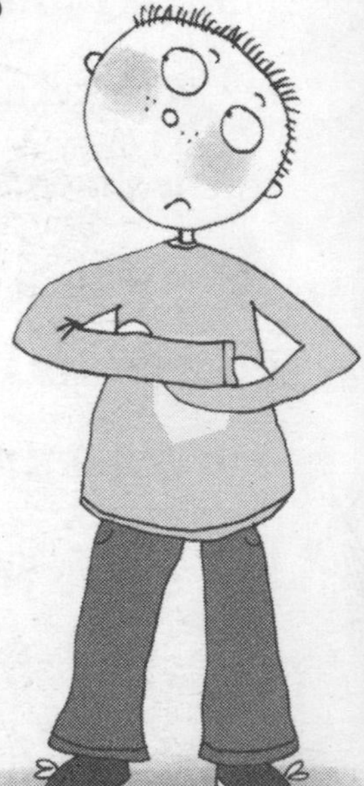

Miss Patterson, who is our teacher, and who is tall and thin like a beanpole, says it would be better if they saved their energy for dancing **NOT** arguing, and also that a mole is not a talent and that Alexander Pringle will have to think of something better, and so he says he is going play "If I Had A Hammer" on his recorder. Only Bridget Grimes says that is **COPYING** and starts crying that he is going to win the prize of a million pounds and it is **NOT FAIR**. Only Miss Patterson says the prize is **NOT** a million pounds, it is a raffia owl and the **JOY** of knowing you have won.

Only Henry Potts says he already has a raffia owl and can the prize be a lightsaber instead and less joy? And I say that would be unfair because I do not want a lightsaber because I am banned from them for several reasons. But Henry Potts says I will not win anyway because I do not have a talent. And I say,

And he says,

And I say,

So he says,

And I say it is an **AMAZING** talent and also **SECRET** because I do not want to be copied by Alexander Pringle. And Henry Potts says I am a **LIAR**. And I say I am not, it is just so **SECRET** that even I do not know what it is yet. So Henry says I am **MAD**.

And Cosmo throws a rubber at him, which is when Miss Patterson says **NO ONE** is mad and **EVERYONE** has talent but that **NO ONE** is going to win any prizes, not even joy and a raffia owl, unless we **PIPE DOWN** and open up our maths books.

So I am utterly racking my head to discover my secret and amazing talent, only I am not discovering anything at all, especially not the answer to "How many buckets of water does it take to fill a bathtub?" (which if you think about it **IS** mad because that is what taps are for). But also I am so busy racking my head that I do not swing on my chair **OR** flick things at Bridget Grimes, so I am not **DREADFUL** and so my new leaf is definitely **TURNING**.

Only when I get home I **STILL** do not know what my secret and amazing talent is and nor does anyone else. Daisy says it is "Being a moron" and Dad does the honking goose laugh, but I do not see the funny side. And nor does Mum who says,

Penelope is
trying **VERY**
hard to turn
over a new leaf,
UNLIKE Daisy,
and if you can't
say something
helpful, Gordon,
don't say
anything
at all.

So Daisy says she is going upstairs to lie on her bed and mope (which is her most favourite activity ever since Mum said she was not allowed a TV in her bedroom not **EVEN** over her dead body), and Dad says, "Did I ever tell you I could have been an Olympic high jumper if I hadn't met your mother." And Mum says, "That is **NOT** what I was thinking of, Gordon, and no you couldn't

because you trip over even a twig."

Which is true because right then Dad tries to high jump, only he trips over the carpet and knocks a big book about bees off the coffee table, which falls on the remote control, which turns off the telly, which is very **FLUMMOXING** for Gran (who has been watching *Animal SOS* about a cow who is trapped in a phone box) who thinks it is maybe magic.

Only Mum says there is no such thing as magic, only **COINCIDENCE**. But Gran says there **IS** such a thing as **MAGIC** because her friend Arthur Peason was a magician called The Great Horrendous, before he got old and bald, and can in fact make rabbits jump out of a hat and also saw people in half. Which is when I have my **BRILLIANT IDEA™**, which is that **MAGIC** can be my secret and amazing talent and it is **SO** amazing that I will definitely win the raffia owl and the joy and also **TURN OVER A NEW LEAF**.

So the next day after school, me and Cosmo and Gran go round to see Arthur Peason

and he puts on his special cloak and hat with silvery stars on it and I am his glamorous assistant and I get inside a special box and he completely saws me in half (because he does not have any rabbits to jump out of a hat any more). Only he does not **ACTUALLY** saw me, he just saws some wood while I am tucked up in a secret compartment.

And then he lets me put on the cloak and hat and I saw Cosmo in half. And then Cosmo says maybe he will not do a sun dance and will be my glamorous assistant instead. Only Arthur Peason says it is very important to have a volunteer from the audience and it absolutely must be a beautiful lady because then the crowd will be on the **EDGE OF THEIR SEATS** and will "ooh" and "aah" a lot more, which is not magic, it is scientific fact.

And then we go home with the box and the saw and the hat and the cloak and I ask Mum to get in the box because she is a beautiful lady, although she is not very voluntary because she says she would quite like to remain in **ONE PIECE** rather than be sawn in two.

Only I say she will not be sawn in two because of the secret compartment and I am right, and so is Arthur Peason because everyone is on the edge of their seats, especially Dad, and they all "ooh" and "aah" and Mum is utterly **NOT** sawn, she is **IN ONE PIECE**, and I am pleased as punch because my leaf has definitely **TURNED**.

★ ★ ★ ★

And on Monday I am so **MAD** with excitement about my secret and amazing talent that I cannot even sit still, and Mr. Schumann has to say, "*Penelope Jones, seats are for bottoms, not for balancing,*" but he does not say he is **SICK AND TIRED** so his new leaf is still turned, even though:

a) Henry Potts has done his rain dance and he has used real rain (i.e. some squeegee bottles) and there is wet on Bridget Grimes's recorder and so she has had to wait a turn until it is all dry, and

2. Alexander Pringle has done his talent, which is not his mole or the recorder, it is fitting marshmallows in his mouth and it is fourteen, only they have fallen out and made a sticky mess on the floor and Mr. Eggs, who is our caretaker and who smells of dog, has had to come and clean it all up.

I say,

Do not worry, Mr. Schumann, because it is my turn next and there is no wet or stick and also I will not be on my seat at all, I will be **AMAZING** you with my secret talent.

And then it is Mr. Schumann's turn to be on the edge of his seat because I am in my hat and cloak and saying, "*I am The Great Cornetto and I am going to saw somebody in half* **MAGICALLY**." Only Mr. Schumann says he does not want anyone being sawn as it is against school rules and also the law. Only I tell him I will not actually saw them because of the secret compartment. And Mr. Schumann checks the secret compartment and says it is definitely there, so I can do some sawing.

And so I say, "*I need a volunteer and they must be beautiful and glamorous*," and everyone is going "*Me, me*" and waving their hands in the air.

Me! Me!

Only I do not think that Cherry Scarpelli is very **GLAMOROUS** because she is dressed like a monkey because her talent is a song from *The Jungle Book*.

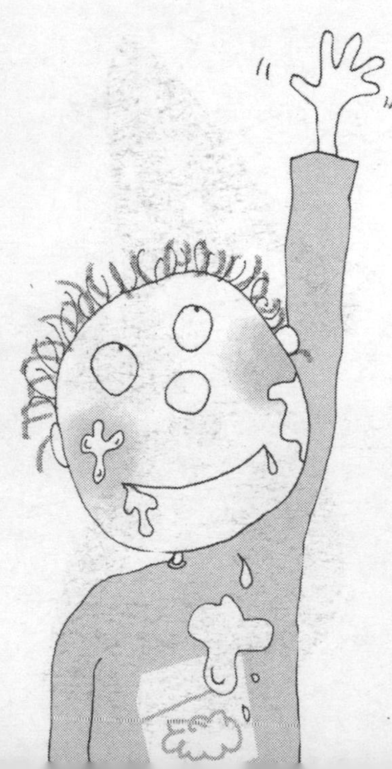

And I do not think Alexander Pringle is very **GLAMOROUS** because he is covered in marshmallow, and also he is not a lady.

And in fact the most **GLAMOROUS** person who is also a lady is Bridget Grimes, because she is wearing a purple dress and also she has long hair that actually reaches her waist and she is always swooshing it and saying "My hair actually reaches my waist, Penelope Jones", only Mum says it needs a jolly good cut. But for once I do not agree because it will be very **GLAMOROUS** when it is hanging out of the box, so I pick her.

And so Bridget is in the box and I am waving my saw and saying,

And it is completely **MAGIC** because I do the

sawing and everyone says,

ooh and aah

like **MAD** and she is completely in **TWO PIECES**.

And then I put her back again and she is

in **ONE PIECE**.

Only that is when the **BAD THING™** happens, which is that I absolutely cannot open the box. And nor can Mr. Schumann, and nor can Miss Patterson, and nor can Mr. Eggs.

And so Mr. Schumann has to call the fire brigade and they do **ACTUAL** sawing to get Bridget Grimes out and there is more "ooh"ing and "aah"ing than ever, and also Bridget Grimes is screaming massively in case they chop her head off with her long hair.

But at last she is **FREE** and everyone claps and the firemen do a bow and everyone is pleased as punch. Except Mr. Schumann, whose leaf has definitely turned the wrong way again because he says he is **SICK AND TIRED** of calling the fire brigade, it is the third time this year,

and I say it is not, it is two, and he says it is definitely three, i.e.:

1. The time I brought Barry in for show-and-tell and he ran up the curtains in the dining hall and got stuck and had to be rescued.

b) The time me and Elsie Maud, who was a new girl but only for a week, got Alexander Pringle to reach a dead pigeon on the other side of the railings and he got his head stuck and had to be rescued.

c) Today.

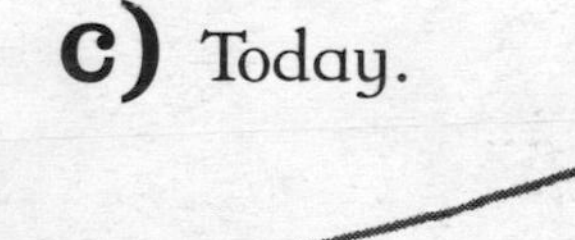

And so he is completely right, which means I am disqualified from the talent show **AND** I am banned from being onstage until I can prove I am responsible, which means I will not get to be a sweetcorn in the Harvest Festival and wear a helmet made of yellow felt. And it means my new leaf has definitely turned back into an old one.

And so has Daisy's, because she is best

friends with Lucy B. Finnegan again since Philippa's TV has been confiscated until she can get at least a B in science, which means Daisy does not have to say Nice Things, she can say what she likes, which right now is,

And Dad calls me Penny Dreadful and does the honking goose laugh, and Mum does not see the funny side.

But for once I do see it. Because even though I do not win, nor does Bridget Grimes, because she is very trembly after the sawing and gets four notes wrong in "If I Had A Hammer" and so she does not show off for at least a week. In fact it is Cosmo who wins with his sun dance, which Mr. Schumann says is at least "dry and tidy".

And even though I am not Cosmo's glamorous assistant, I am utterly his best friend, and so he says I can share half his joy and have the raffia owl every other weekend.

Penny Dreadful
and the
Birthday
Wish

Mostly I do not see the point of wishes because they absolutely almost **NEVER** come true. For instance, so far this year I have wished for:

a) A butterscotch ice cream that never melts

b) A Tyrannosaurus rex

3. A pair of X-ray glasses

4. A time machine (for Cosmo's birthday because he is very keen on time machines, especially ones made out of a bus, some tinfoil and an alarm clock)

v) £43.82

And I did not get a butterscotch ice cream that never melts, or a pair of X-ray glasses or a Tyrannosaurus rex. And Cosmo did not get his time machine, he got some liquorice sticks and a pen in the shape of a vampire.

But he was pleased as punch anyway because Henry Potts, who is his mortal enemy, has a pen in the shape of a werewolf and Cosmo says vampires are more deadly than werewolves and his pen would obliterate Henry Potts's pen, which it did, only Miss Patterson was not very happy about all the ink on the floor, which Cosmo said was werewolf blood,

which made Bridget Grimes
cry because she thinks
werewolves are real
(but I have checked
with Mr. Schumann
and they are not, they
are only on television
and in America).

But I am **NOT** pleased as punch, especially about the £43.82 because that is how much I owe Mum for a lot of reasons, e.g.:

1. The time I accidentally called India.

b) The time we broke Dad's razor by shaving Georgia May Morton-Jones's head which had superglue on it.

iii) The time me and Cosmo broke the vacuum cleaner by sucking up some bubbles.

And I will be paying her back **UNTIL KINGDOM COME**, only I wish it would come quickish because it is Mum's birthday **TODAY** and I need £3.99 to buy her a mug with a picture of a monkey on it that is in the window at the post office, so I can

give it to her at her **BIRTHDAY TEA** later.

Mum says she would rather just have some **PEACE** and **QUIET** because at that **EXACT** moment Daisy and Lucy B. Finnegan are standing on the table pretending to be international horse riders receiving Olympic medals for jumping over some red and white planks and they are **LOUD**, and Gran is watching the news which is about some bombs exploding which are very **LOUD**, and Barry the cat is howling (only it is not because of the bombs but because he does not like the man who does the news) and he is quite **LOUD**, and I am saying,

But if you do not lend me some money then I cannot buy you a present and you will be doubly cross with me and so you see it is completely not my fault.

And I am saying it quite **LOUD**. So Mum says she is just glad that Dad is still out at work solving a crisis to do with a roundabout because at least it is one less noise to add to the **CACOPHONY**. Which is when Dad walks in and adds his noise to the **CACOPHONY** by saying,

The roundabout is fixed, no thanks to Kenny Jupiter, honestly, he has baked beans for brains – oh and I hope you don't mind but I have invited Deedee over for **BIRTHDAY TEA** later and it will be absolutely fun, you will see.

Only I think that possibly Mum **WILL NOT** see and she **WILL** mind because Aunt Deedee is almost **NEVER** fun and almost **ALWAYS** getting cross with me or Mum or Gran, e.g. for accidentally letting Georgia May Morton-Jones, who is my cousin and who is four and a bit and goes to The Drabble Academy for Girls, eat mud.

And I am right because Mum says she **WISHES** Dad would learn to think before he speaks or that a fairy godmother would appear and whisk her away to Timbuktu or even just to Chipping Broadley, as long as it is very far from all this **HOO-HA**.

But until that happens she is going to the hairdresser's for a **BIRTHDAY TRIM** and Shaniqua Reynolds had better not be **OVERAMBITIOUS**. And I am about to say that statistically I do not think her **WISH** will happen because I have still not got my Tyrannosaurus or the butterscotch ice cream that never melts or a pair of X-ray glasses, only then I remember about the **PEACE** and **QUIET** so I go to Cosmo's house instead.

★ ★ ★ ★

Cosmo's house is good because his mum, who is called Sunflower (even though her real name is Barbara), does not believe in **PEACE** and **QUIET**, she believes in **FREE SPEECH** because it is Cosmo's **HUMAN RIGHT**, even if the speech is being Darth Vader and saying "*I am Darth Vader and I am going to smite you with my omnipotent powers*" a hundred and forty-three times (which is what he did last Sunday). But today he is not keen on being Darth Vader, he is keen on swapping a rubber in the shape of a weasel for my Dogs of the World poster. This is because at school everyone is **MAD** for swaps, e.g.:

a) Alexander Pringle has swapped a jam sandwich for Luke Bruce's peanut butter biscuit.

b) Bridget Grimes has swapped a broken Barbie doll for Cherry Scarpelli's My Little Pony with the tail cut off.

3. Brady O'Grady has swapped a shiny fifty pence for Denzil Wellington's one pound coin with a dent in it.

d) Henry Potts has swapped Optimus Prime, leader of the Autobots, for Jamal Malik's little brother Shoaib, only Shoaib is not very happy about this and nor is Mrs. Malik and nor is Mr. Schumann who decides to ban swaps at school until we can learn what is swappable and what is not.

So I say I will not swap my Dogs of the World poster for Cosmo's rubber in the shape of a weasel but I **WILL** swap a tin of sardines that is past its use-by date (and which Gran was going to give to Barry) for the rubber, and Cosmo says

yes because the tin might be an antique and worth a fortune e.g. £50 in five years' time, and we can go on telly and everyone will **GASP** and wish they had kept their tin of sardines.

And I say it is a shame it is not five years' time now because then I could sell the tin of sardines and pay Mum back £43.82 **AND** buy her the mug with the monkey on it from the post office, as it is only £3.99. Which is when Cosmo has a

BRILLIANT IDEA™,

which is to not **BUY** the mug but to **SWAP** something for it with Mrs. Butterworth who works in the post office and who has a moustache and a beady eye (which I know because she is mostly saying "*I have got my beady eye on you, Penelope Jones*").

So we are investigating Cosmo's **WORLDLY POSSESSIONS**, i.e. the contents of his cupboard with the wonky handle, for something good to swap and we find seven things and they are:

1. A pair of stilts made out of flower pots

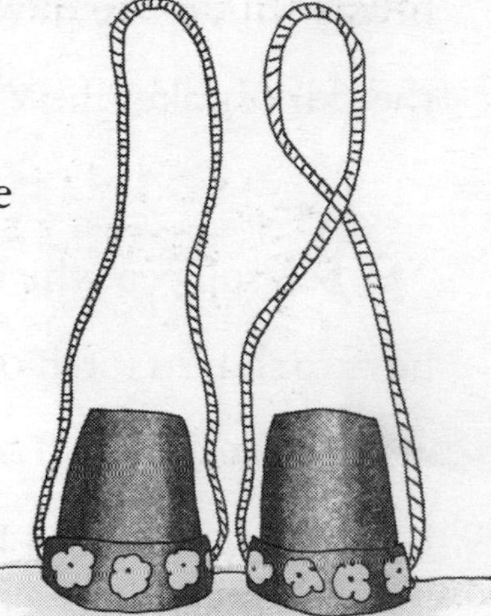

2. Buckingham Palace on a key ring

c) A dried toad

d) A snow globe of Rapunzel that is leaky and all the snow is on the carpet

V. Three baby teeth

6. A book about deadly beasts with a free glow-in-the-dark snake ring

g) A spy pen which uses invisible ink and you have to shine a torch on it to see what is written and once we wrote "*Henry Potts eats woodlice*" on his spelling book and Henry **STILL** hasn't seen it, which Cosmo says is **BRILLIANT** but I say is disappointing because where is the fun in **THAT**?

Cosmo says Mrs. Butterworth will not want the snow globe of Rapunzel that is leaky with all the snow on the carpet, or three baby teeth, or a book about deadly beasts with a free glow-in-the-dark snake ring. Which means she is **MAD**, because who would **NOT** want a book about beasts with a free glow-in-the-dark snake ring?

★ ★ ★ ★

Anyway it turns out she is **DOUBLY MAD**, because she also does not want the pair of stilts made out of flowerpots **OR** the Buckingham Palace on a key ring **OR** the dried toad **OR** the spy pen with invisible ink, and in fact she does not want to swap the mug with the monkey on it that is only £3.99

for **ANYTHING**, except £3.99 in **ACTUAL** money and **NOT** in foreign coins. And Cosmo says,

which is when you write down e.g.:

> I OWE you four pieces of cola flavoured bubble gum

on a piece of paper and give it to Alexander Pringle. Only Alexander Pringle says he is not falling for that again because Cosmo still owes him for the gum, and Mrs. Butterworth says **SHE** is not falling for that again because Mr. Nugent still owes her for a first-class stamp and a packet of Gypsy Creams and she will never get that back because he perished in 1997. I say I am absolutely **NOT** going to perish but Mrs. Butterworth gives me a look with her beady eye that could quite possibly perish me anyway, so me and Cosmo are back at **SQUARE ONE** (which is also called Cosmo's house).

And we are lying on his rug made out of recycled shopping bags and saying,

quite a lot when Sunflower comes in, and she is very **KEEN** on fairness so we tell her about the **BIRTHDAY TEA** and Timbuktu and the mug with the monkey on it (which is only £3.99), only Sunflower says a mug with a monkey on it is **NOT** a good present because it is a **BOUGHT** present and all the best presents are ones that are made with **LOVE** or recycled shopping bags.

But Cosmo says we do not **HAVE** any recycled shopping bags because she made them into a poncho last week, so it will have to be **LOVE**. Only I say it will have to be some **LOVE** that does not involve scissors or glue because I am **BANNED** from them for several reasons. And Sunflower says in that case I can bake my **LOVE** into a **CAKE**, which will make Mum utterly pleased and she will not want to go to Timbuktu **OR** Chipping Broadley and we can make it right here which is **FORTUITOUS** because I am not allowed to use the cooker at our house.

But what is **NOT FORTUITOUS** is that Sunflower does not believe in **RECIPES** because they are like **RULES** and rules are against her **HUMAN RIGHTS** and she says we have to use our

IMAGINATIONS and invent a **CAKE OF DREAMS**.

So what we do is we get a giant bowl and in it we put several things from the cupboard, i.e.:

1. A bag of flour

b. A box of eggs

c. A jar of black treacle

4. Some cubes of lime jelly, cut up

5. A packet of chocolate buttons

f. Some grated cheese (because Mum is always saying that grated cheese is the **ICING ON THE CAKE** of **ANY** food, but we put it **INSIDE** the cake because we want to put pink stuff and some plastic farm animals on top).

And that is when I have my

BRILLIANT IDEA™,

which is to put a coin inside the cake too and it will be like the lucky 20p in the Christmas pudding and whoever gets it will be able to make a special wish, e.g. for a year's supply of digestive biscuits, and Cosmo says that is definitely a

BRILLIANT IDEA™.

Only we cannot find a coin so we have to use a plastic piglet instead, but Cosmo says it is definitely a lucky piglet because it only has three legs but it can still stand up, which is a **MIRACLE**.

So then we go to the garden and ask Sunflower to turn the oven on (because she is doing yoga by the compost and because we are being **RESPONSIBLE** and also because Cosmo does not know which knob is **ON**), and we put the cake inside for almost about an hour which is when Cosmo says it must definitely be absolutely cooked by now.

And he is right because mostly it has risen up like **MAD**, except for the middle which is very sunken and also a bit gloopy, plus the three-legged piglet is upside down in it and it looks like it has drowned in some mud, but Cosmo says we will cover that up with the pink stuff and no one will be **ANY THE WISER**.

And he is right again, because we put on loads of pink stuff, which is made from butter and sugar and beetroot juice for the pink (because Sunflower does not believe in **ARTIFICIAL COLOURING**), and we stick a cow and a horse with one eye on top and it looks **MAGNIFICENT** and is utterly a **CAKE OF DREAMS**.

And then we carry it completely carefully all the way back to my house for the **BIRTHDAY TEA**.

And when we get there Mum is already looking utterly gloomy and also very strange because Shaniqua Reynolds has definitely been **OVERAMBITIOUS** and now her hair is definitely shorter on one side than the other and Dad is saying,

Only Mum says,

Gordon, if you cannot say anything helpful then do not say anything at all.

So then he is utterly quiet. But someone is **NOT** utterly quiet and that is Aunt Deedee who says,

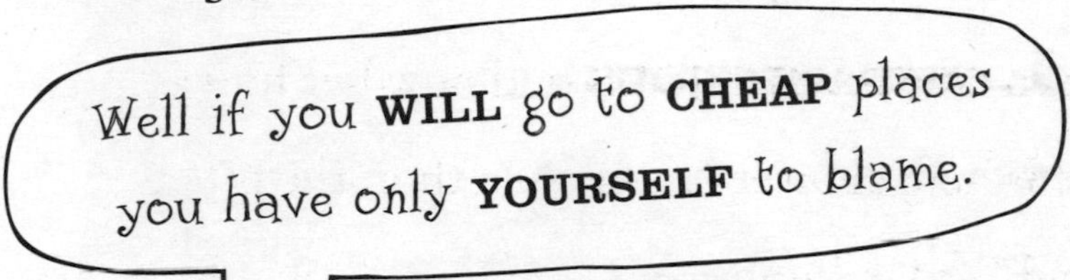

Well if you **WILL** go to **CHEAP** places you have only **YOURSELF** to blame.

Because she goes to Antonio's in Chipping Broadley and it is £50 for just a haircut, which Aunt Deedee says is **MONEY WELL SPENT** but which normally Mum says is **MADNESS** and she is the one who is smiling (only she is not smiling now).

So then Dad says, "Maybe it is present time," and everyone agrees and so Mum opens her presents, which are:

1. Some oven gloves from Dad.

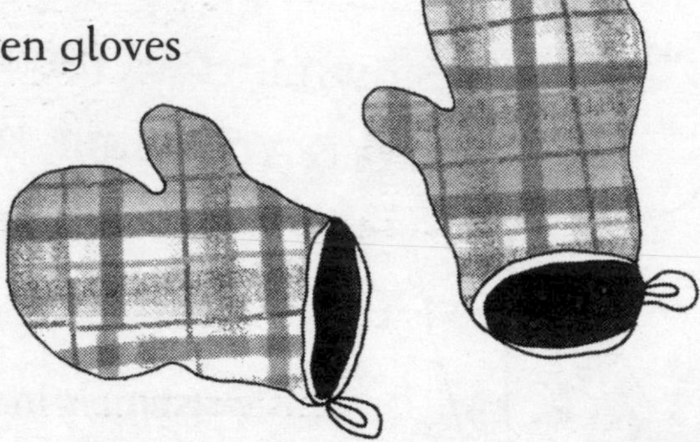

b) A purple scarf from Daisy because purple is Daisy's favourite colour this week.

c) A bottle of rum from Gran.

4. A book about birds from Barry.

5. A ticket to a concert by Mr. Nakamura (who is Georgia May Morton-Jones's music teacher and says she shows potential on the violin) from Aunt Deedee.

And Daisy says,

And I say, "It is **NOT**, it is a **CAKE OF DREAMS** and it is the best kind of present because it is made with **LOVE**, and also eggs and some other stuff, and here it is – **TA-DA**!" And me and Cosmo bring in the **CAKE OF DREAMS** and put it on the table.

And Daisy says,
Why is there a horse with one eye on top?
And Cosmo says,
It is **DECORATION**, and also there is a three-legged pig inside and whoever gets it can make a wish.
And Dad says,
Splendid. What a **BRILLIANT IDEA™**!

Only Mum is not looking as if she thinks it is completely **BRILLIANT** but that is only because she has not tasted it yet, so I say,

And so Dad does it because I am not allowed to use a knife ever since the time I sliced a very little bit of my thumb off. And there is a piece

for everyone except Barry (because Mum says it is **CAT BISCUITS AND  CAT BISCUITS ONLY**).

Only Aunt Deedee possibly wishes there wasn't a piece for her because almost immediately she goes very palish and then very reddish and it is clear she is **CHOKING**.

And so Cosmo says,

Do not fear,
I will come to your rescue, I am your
KNIGHT IN SHINING ARMOUR.

Because he is very keen on being a knight in shining armour (as well as Darth Vader). And he hits her very hard on the back, which is when the three-legged piglet flies out and hits Dad on the nose.

And then there is all sorts of **KERFUFFLE** and Aunt Deedee is completely cross and goes home to be **REVIVED** with the bottle of rum, and then there is shouting of,

And especially that it is **MY** fault because I am such a **COMPLETE MORON** and it is the worst birthday **EVER** (it is Daisy who says that).

But **AMAZINGLY** Mum does not agree and she is smiling, even though her hair is wonky. And she says in fact it is the **BEST** birthday ever because she got her **WISH**, which is that Aunt Deedee would **BE QUIET** and **GO HOME**. And I absolutely agree that it is the **BEST BIRTHDAY EVER** because at that exact moment Dad finds another present under the table and he says, "*Oh, is this from you too, Penny?*" And I say, "*No.*" And he says, "*Yes it is, it says so here.*"

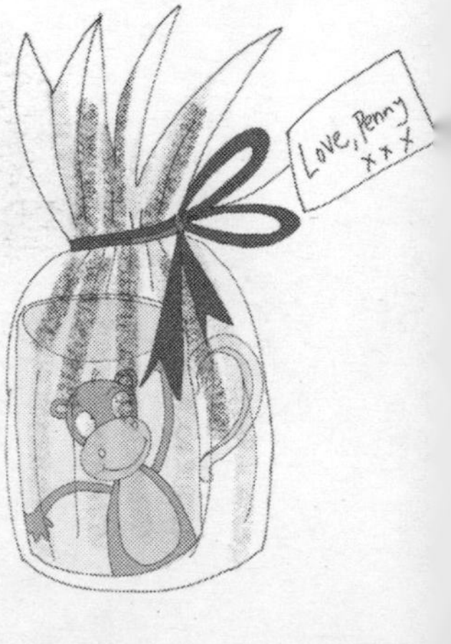

And Mum opens it and it is the mug with the monkey on it from the post office and Dad gives me a wink and I give him a wink back and I think that maybe wishes **DO** come true after all.

Penny Dreadful
and the
School Outing
DO NOT OPEN
Mummified Cat

Mr. Schumann is our headmaster

and he is mostly saying things like "Penelope Jones, I am **SICK** and **TIRED** of telling you to stop putting that pencil up your nose", which is not even true because it was a biro and plus I was only seeing if I could get the raisin out that was stuck in there from lunchtime, which I could, so it was a **GOOD THING**. But he is also saying something else absolutely a lot, which is "*The world is* **FULL OF WONDER** *so you must be* **FULL OF WONDER** *too*".

And mostly me and Cosmo Moon Webster are not in agreement with him, because we do not see what is so **WONDERFUL** about our village which does not have, e.g.:

1. A mysterious and ancient burial ground
b) Smugglers
c) A Tyrannosaurus rex
4. Darth Vader

Instead it has a park with a broken swing (from when me and Cosmo were doing an experiment to see how many people could fit on it before it broke and it was four), a dead pigeon that has been behind the post office for two weeks and no one has moved it, and a one-way system that Dad says **BEGGARS BELIEF**.

And so I tell Miss Patterson, who is our teacher and who is tall and thin like a beanpole, that my world is absolutely **NOT** full of **WONDER** and that in fact it **BEGGARS BELIEF**, but she says Mr. Schumann was not talking about this exact village, and that I need to look further than **IN FRONT OF MY EYES** and I will see all sorts of interesting things, e.g. the **WONDERS OF THE WORLD** and there are seven of them.

And then everyone is arguing like **MAD** about what the **WONDERS OF THE WORLD** are, i.e.:

1. Bridget Grimes says one is the Queen's Palace.

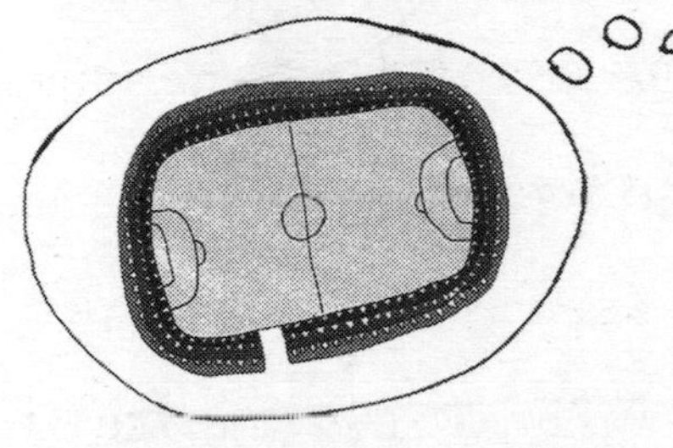

2. Brady O'Grady says one is Bronstonworth United Football Ground.

c) Henry Potts says one is Alexander Pringle, because he wears age 14 clothes even though he is nine (which is because of his glands, and also the eating).

d) Cosmo says one is Henry Potts's brain because it is so small, even smaller than a flea poo, and not even a microscope can see it.

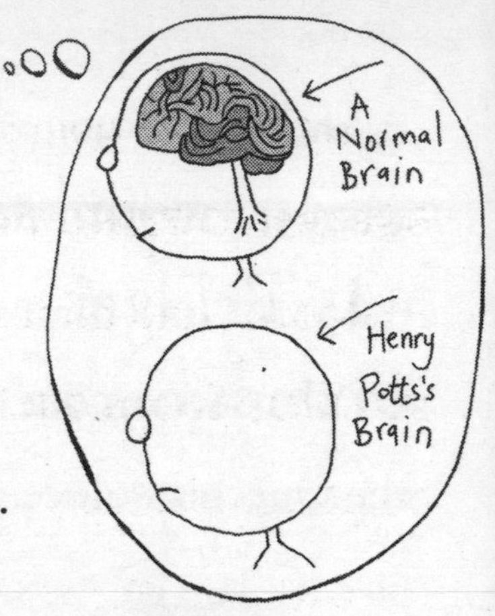

But Miss Patterson says we are all wrong because in fact they are:

a) The Hanging Gardens of Babylon
b) The Great Pyramid of Giza
3. The Mausoleum of Halicarnassus
iv) The Temple of Artemis
5. The Colossus of Rhodes
f) The Statue of Zeus
7. The Lighthouse of Alexandria

And we are going to see one of them on a **SCHOOL OUTING** tomorrow and it is a **PYRAMID** and almost immediately I am **FULL OF WONDER** because I am very **KEEN** on pyramids, especially the **CURSE OF THE MUMMIES**, which means that when you go into a mummy's tomb they put an ancient **CURSE** on you and you will **PERISH**, which I tell Miss Patterson.

Only then Bridget Grimes starts crying because she does not want to be cursed by the mummies and perish, and Cherry Scarpelli is crying because she does not want to go to Egypt and get a bad tummy like she did in Benidorm last year, and Brady O'Grady is crying because Alexander Pringle stamped on his foot because Brady said Alexander was the Colossus of St Regina's.

Which is when Miss Patterson says to all stop being **SILLY** because **NO ONE** is going to **EGYPT** and **NO ONE** is going to get **CURSED** because we are going to the Chipping Broadley Museum to look at a piece of sarcophagus and a mummified cat and some photos of the Great Pyramid and it is five pounds for the bus and you must wear **STRICT UNIFORM AND UNIFORM ONLY** and also get your mum or dad to sign the special form or you will be staying behind to pick up litter with Mr. Eggs (who is our caretaker and who smells of dog).

And so when I get home I tell Mum about the **WORLD OF WONDER** and that she absolutely has to sign the special form and give me five pounds (especially because Mr. Eggs does not like me since the time I accidentally clogged the sink by trying to wash some semolina away). And Mum says,

Hmmm, I suppose it will be mind-expanding, but there will have to be **RULES**, Penelope Jones.

And they are:

1. No **SHENANIGANS** on the bus

2. No getting **LOST**

c) No **TOUCHING** artefacts, which are old and ancient things in museums

Because she does **NOT** want to be paying for more **BREAKAGES**, because she has only just paid the man at the Chocolate Museum for the time I ate a bit of the Caramel Crunch Leaning Tower of Pisa, which in fact was not my fault, it was Cosmo's, because he is the one who said it would make it less leany. Only I do not say this, I say **YES** I will **NOT** do any of those things, and so she signs the form.

Daisy says,

But I say I will not be a moron because I will be too busy being **FULL OF WONDER** and she is just jealous because she wishes **SHE** was going to look at artefacts instead of doing double maths with Mr. Munnings who has hairy hands.

And Daisy says that is not true and I say **IS** and she says **IS NOT** and I say **IS** and we do that a lot until Mum says she wishes **SHE** was going to look at artefacts instead of looking after us lot, which is a **THANKLESS TASK**. And then Dad says he wishes **HE** was going to look at artefacts instead of having a meeting about the yellow lines outside the Scout Hut, which are causing all sorts of hoo-ha with the Akela, because that is a **THANKLESS TASK**. And Gran says she wishes **SHE** was coming to look at artefacts instead of playing Beetle Drive with Arthur Peason because that is a **THANKLESS TASK** because he always cheats. Which is when Mum says that none of us understand the meaning of **THANKLESS**, and to please stop the artefact nonsense because she has had it **UP TO HERE** today, what with Dr. Cement and his broken door handle, which meant he got trapped in his office with Mrs. Nougat and her bunions for an **HOUR**. So then we are all as quiet as **MICE** and no one mentions artefacts again, not **EVEN** in a whisper.

★ ★ ★ ★

But the next morning when I go to school everyone is **MAD** with **EXCITEMENT** about the artefacts, except Luke Bruce who has forgotten his form and so it is litter-picking with Mr. Eggs for him. Miss Patterson says it is also litter-picking for Cosmo because he is not in **STRICT UNIFORM**, only Cosmo says he has his form and it **IS** signed and so is a letter from his mum Sunflower which says that she does not believe in **UNIFORM** because it is oppressive and made of polyester, and she believes in **FREEDOM** and **SELF-EXPRESSION** and also natural fibres, which is why he is wearing a turban and a big cloak.

And Miss Patterson does not have anything to say to that, which is a **GOOD THING**, because if she did, Sunflower would have a one-woman sit-in protest because she is very **KEEN** on them (but Miss Patterson and Mr. Schumann are not).

And also because at that very minute Dwayne Eggs, who is the son of Mr. Eggs (but does not smell of dog), arrives driving the bus, and it is **NOT** the old one that smells of sick, it is a **NEW** one called the Speedy Superbus and it has a machine for drinks and one for crisps and a toilet and a shower and a sprinkler system in case of **FIRE** and a stop lever in case of **EMERGENCIES** and in fact Dwayne Eggs says it is a **WONDER OF THE WORLD**.

Only Bridget Grimes says no it is not, because she has learned them all by heart and she will tell him if he wants, only Dwayne Eggs does not want, and nor does Mr. Schumann, who says it is time to climb on board and that we must absolutely be on our **BEST BEHAVIOUR** or we will let all sorts of people down, e.g.:

a) Miss Patterson

2. St Regina's

c) **OURSELVES**

And he looks especially at me at that bit. I say,

"I have **NEVER** let myself down." And Mr. Schumann says, "Two out of three is bad enough." But I do not understand what he means so instead I just climb on board and Miss Patterson counts us all and there are twenty-seven and Mr. Schumann says there had better be twenty-seven on the way back or it will be **CURTAINS** for school outings.

So at last we are **OFF** and Mr. Schumann was right because I am absolutely **FULL OF WONDER** and it is at the Speedy Superbus. And I am wondering whether to have a shower first or get a can of lemonade and Cosmo says it is best to have the lemonade first because then if I make a mess I can shower the lemony all off.

And it is completely **FORTUITOUS** because Mum has given me a one pound coin, only it is to get something from the museum shop with or for **EMERGENCIES**, but I think the lemonade is maybe an **EMERGENCY** because I am super-thirsty and Cosmo has used my water to make a swimming pool for a fly which is on the floor.

So I put my coin in the slot, only a can of lemonade **DOES NOT** come out. Which completely **BEGGARS BELIEF** and is also a definite **EMERGENCY**, so I think I had better pull the **EMERGENCY STOP LEVER**, only at that exact moment Bridget Grimes appears and she says, "*I would not do that if I were you, Penelope Jones, or you will be letting yourself* **DOWN**." And so I say, "*I would not say 'I would not do that if I were you', Bridget Grimes, because* **YOU** *are letting* **YOURSELF** *down.*"

And then everyone goes mad with who is letting who down, e.g.:

a) Brady O'Grady says if Cherry Scarpelli does not give him a Murray Mint then she is letting **PRINCE WILLIAM** down (because she is very **KEEN** on Prince William).

ii) Cosmo says if Henry Potts does not stick his hand in the fly swimming pool then he is letting **ALL THE INSECTS IN THE WORLD** down.

3. Henry Potts says if Cosmo does not sacrifice himself to Optimus Prime then he will be letting **THE AUTOBOTS** down.

And then Bridget Grimes is crying because she has slid over on the fly swimming pool and knocked her head on the lemonade machine, which makes a pingy noise and my one pound coin falls out, which is a **MIRACLE** and I say,

Which is when Miss Patterson says in fact we are **ALL** letting **HER** down and if we do not sit down and also stop fiddling with things then Dwayne Eggs will turn the **SPEEDY SUPERBUS** round this very minute and it will be litter-picking for all of us. And **NO ONE** is very pleased about this, especially Dwayne, who says he is meeting his friend Ant the Plank in Chipping Broadley so he will not be turning anything round until at least half past eleven. So we do all sit down and I don't even test the sprinkler system in case of **FIRE** although I would very much like to.

But when we get to the museum I am glad I did not do any testing because almost immediately I am **FULL OF WONDER**, because right inside the front door is a real actual stuffed walrus and I am very **KEEN** on walruses (because they have tusks, and skin like Mrs. Butterworth at the post office or like leather handbags). And I am just about to stroke it to see if it feels like Mrs. Butterworth or a handbag, because Mum did not say I could not **STROKE** artefacts,

when Miss Patterson says, "Do not even **THINK** about it, Penelope Jones, we are not here to look at walruses, we are here to look at a cat and a coffin in a glass case," which is what we do.

And it is excellent because the room is gold and quite dark and Cosmo says it is definitely cursed with an **ANCIENT** and **TERRIBLE** spell and if Henry Potts even **LOOKS** at the cat his nose will fall off. So Henry Potts says if Cosmo even **LOOKS** at the cat his **EAR** will fall off. And Brady O'Grady says if Alexander Pringle even **LOOKS** at the cat his **HEAD** will fall off. And then Bridget Grimes starts crying again because she **HAS LOOKED** at the cat already and she is worrying that everything is going to fall off **ANY MINUTE**.

DO NOT OPEN
Mummified Cat

And in fact the only person who is not **CRYING** or **GETTING CURSED** is me, which means I am not letting anyone down and Mr. Schumann would be utterly **PLEASED AS PUNCH** because I am absolutely also doing definite **WONDERING**, e.g.:

And so in fact I **DO** open the lid of the glass cabinet and what happens is an **ALARM** goes off and a man in a hat comes in and says,

And I say in fact I can but I did not see the sign because I was too **FULL OF WONDER**.

Which is when Miss Patterson says we are **ALL** letting her down, except for **ME** because I have let **MYSELF** down too, and it is back to the big room with the walrus after all.

And then Henry Potts is moaning because he says walruses with tusks are not as full of **WONDER** as cats with curses. Only Cosmo says his mum Sunflower says **EVERYTHING** is full of **WONDER**, even things like mud, you just have to **LOOK PROPERLY**. And Miss Patterson says for once Sunflower is right, and Cosmo is **PLEASED AS PUNCH** because that almost never happens.

And then he is **DOUBLY** pleased because Miss Patterson says everyone has to find something that is **INTERESTING** in the big room and write it down and Mr. Schumann can be the judge of which is **MOST** interesting when we get back, only there is to be **NO OPENING OF CABINETS**. And then everyone is running around like **MAD** but **NOT OPENING CABINETS** and we are finding all sorts of interesting things, e.g.:

a) A monkey with his eye fallen out
b) A bent coin
3. Half a fossilized fish

But I am still absolutely **INTERESTED** in the walrus and it is not **EVEN** in a cabinet so I think I will just stroke it now because Mr. Schumann will utterly want to know if it feels like Mrs. Butterworth. Only then something definitely **CURSED** happens which is that a tusk just **FALLS OFF** and I didn't even wiggle it more than two times. And so I am about to stick it back in the hole in the walrus's mouth when I see the man with the hat coming completely quickly in my direction, so I think it is not a good time to be sticking tusks back on walruses (even ones that have not been glued properly) and so I put it in my pocket for later and go completely quickly in the other direction to look at a knife with a ruby in the handle.

Only what happens is I am so **FULL OF WONDER** at the knife with the ruby in the handle that I completely forget about the tusk. And when Miss Patterson says it is time to get back on the Speedy Superbus and there had better be twenty-seven of us and I can do the counting as I absolutely need to practise my maths, I am so **FULL OF WONDER** at being allowed to count that I completely forget about the tusk again.

★ ★ ★ ★

Only when we get back to school it also turns out that I forgot about Alexander Pringle who was in the museum shop buying a rubber shaped like a beehive. Only I still counted to twenty-seven people which I say is a **CURSE**, but which Miss Patterson says is an **OVERSIGHT** and it is not the same thing and it is because I counted her by mistake and so she is **SICK AND TIRED**.

And Dwayne Eggs is **SICK AND TIRED** because he has to go back to Chipping Broadley on the Superbus to fetch Alexander Pringle, only he wants to play Nintendo. But the most **SICK AND TIRED** is Mr. Schumann when I ask if Dwayne can possibly take back the walrus tusk that I have just miraculously found in my pocket as well. He says it is **CURTAINS** for school outings until I can learn to count and also to not meddle with museum exhibits and no I have not won the "most interesting" competition, Cherry Scarpelli has won it with a bucket made of bronze.

Daisy says, "*It is all your fault, Penelope Jones, you are such a complete* **MORON**." Only I say I am not a **MORON**. I am just **TOO FULL OF WONDER**. And sometimes that is an utter **CURSE**.

And for once Mum agrees.

Penny Dreadful's Top 5 Tips for Survival

Sometimes it is very **ARDUOUS** being a **MAGNET FOR DISASTER**. Especially if you are extra specially magnetic, i.e. like me. But even though it is **ARDUOUS**, it is also very **INFORMATIVE**, i.e. I have learned some important **TOP TIPS** about how to avoid complete **CATASTROPHE**.

Number 1

Get a **DISGUISE**

It is completely important not to look like me, i.e. Penelope Jones, when I am being very magnetic, e.g. accidentally knocking over a teetering pile of envelopes in the post office. So sometimes I dress up as Cosmo, i.e. in a Jedi outfit and wellies, because it completely confuses Mrs. Butterworth's beady eye and however hard she **RACKS** her brain she is **FLUMMOXED** as to who to shout at.

Another good disguise is dressing up as a burglar, because burglars wear balaclavas which **COMPLETELY** cover up their face.

Although it is possible you would get shouted at for being a burglar anyway.

Number 2

Collect COLLATERAL, i.e. money

Coins are **EVERYWHERE**, e.g. on the ground outside the post office, down the back of the sofa and mostly in Dad's trouser pocket.

Collect them **ALL** because you never know when you might need them for:

1. Paying people back, e.g. your Aunt Deedee when you have accidentally broken a glass vase or phoned Russia for instance.

b) Buying essential supplies like biscuits or liquorice sticks.

iii. Playing ludo, because you have used the actual plastic counters to flick at your mortal enemy.

Number 3

Be PREPARED for EVERY EVENTUALITY

DISASTERS are **EVERYWHERE** and you never know when you might be super-magnetic, so it is completely important to have a box of useful things for **EVERY EVENTUALITY**, i.e. anything, e.g.:

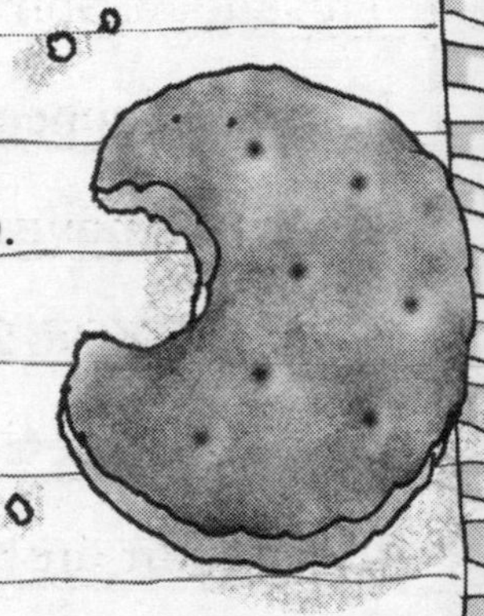

a) **COLLATERAL** (see above).

2. **A DISGUISE** (see above).

3. Biscuits (for **ARDUOUS JOURNEYS**).

4. A bottle of washing-up liquid and a sponge (for when you have spilled something, or accidentally drawn some Roman soldiers marching along the kitchen wall).

e) A torch (for when you have accidentally blown up the vacuum cleaner by trying to suck up the washing-up liquid, and all the lights have gone off).

Number 4

Find a **TRUSTY SCAPEGOAT**

This means someone else to **BLAME**, e.g. in our house everyone mostly blames me, even though it is not usually my fault, it is that I am a **MAGNET FOR DISASTER**. So I usually blame Barry the cat, because he is most often eating things that are **NOT** cat biscuits. E.g. when Daisy said, "Where is my last cherry chocolate, Penelope Jones? I **KNOW** it is you who has eaten it," I said, "But in fact perhaps it is not I, it is **BARRY**, because he is completely **KEEN** on cherries and chocolate, so ha!"

Number 5

Get a FAITHFUL FRIEND

If you are very magnetic like me, it is **COMPLETELY** important to have a faithful friend, which is not the same thing as a scapegoat, and is also not the same as a dog, (especially not one that isn't yours but which you have found outside the post office only it is not lost at all) but e.g. Cosmo Moon Webster. Because faithful friends will always stand up for you, even when you have accidentally exploded custard in their microwave, and even if they are a boy and exactly a week older than you.

My Faithful Friend

Joanna Nadin

wrote this book – and lots of others like it. She is small, funny, clever, sneaky and musical.

Before she became a writer, she wanted to be a champion ballroom dancer or a jockey, but she was actually a lifeguard at a swimming pool, a radio newsreader, a cleaner in an old people's home, and a juggler. She likes Marmite on toast for mains breakfast, and jam on toast for pudding. Her perfect day would involve baking, surfing, sitting in cafes in Paris, and playing with her daughter – who reminds her a lot of Penny Dreadful...

Jess Mikhail

illustrated this book.

She loves creating funny characters with bright colours and fancy patterns to make people smile.

Her favourite place is her tiny home, where she lives with her tiny dog and spends lots of time drawing, scanning, scribbling, printing, stamping, and sometimes using her scary computer. She loves to rummage through a good car boot sale or a charity shop to find weird and wonderful things. A perfect day for her would have to involve a sunny beach and large amounts of curry and ice cream (not together).

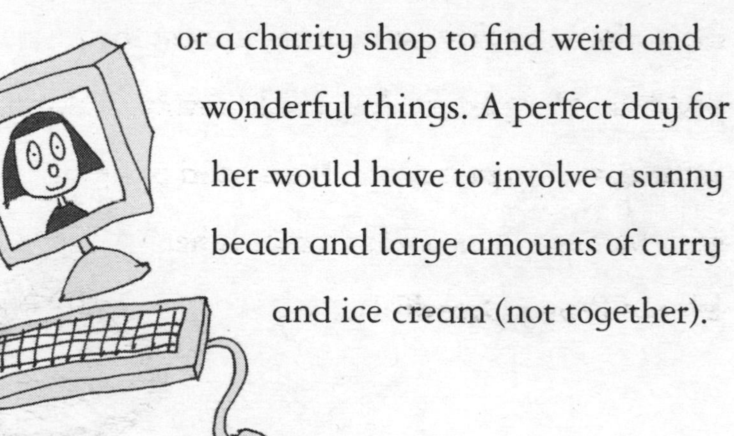

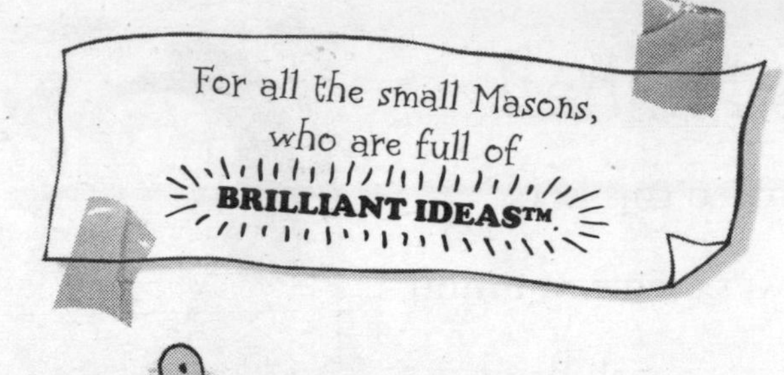

First published in the UK in 2012 by Usborne Publishing Ltd., Usborne House,
83-85 Saffron Hill, London EC1N 8RT, England. www.usborne.com

Copyright © Joanna Nadin, 2012
Illustrations copyright © Usborne Publishing Ltd., 2012

The right of Joanna Nadin to be identified as the author of this work has been asserted by her in accordance with the Copyright, Designs and Patents Act, 1988.

The name Usborne and the devices are Trade Marks of Usborne Publishing Ltd.

All rights reserved. No part of this publication may be reproduced, stored in a retrieval system or transmitted in any form or by any means, electronic, mechanical, photocopying, recording or otherwise without the prior permission of the publisher.
This is a work of fiction. The characters, incidents, and dialogues are products of the author's imagination and are not to be construed as real. Any resemblance to actual events or persons, living or dead, is entirely coincidental.

A CIP catalogue record for this book is available from the British Library.

JFMA JJASOND/12

ISBN 9781409540526 00843/1
Printed in Reading, Berkshire, UK.